The

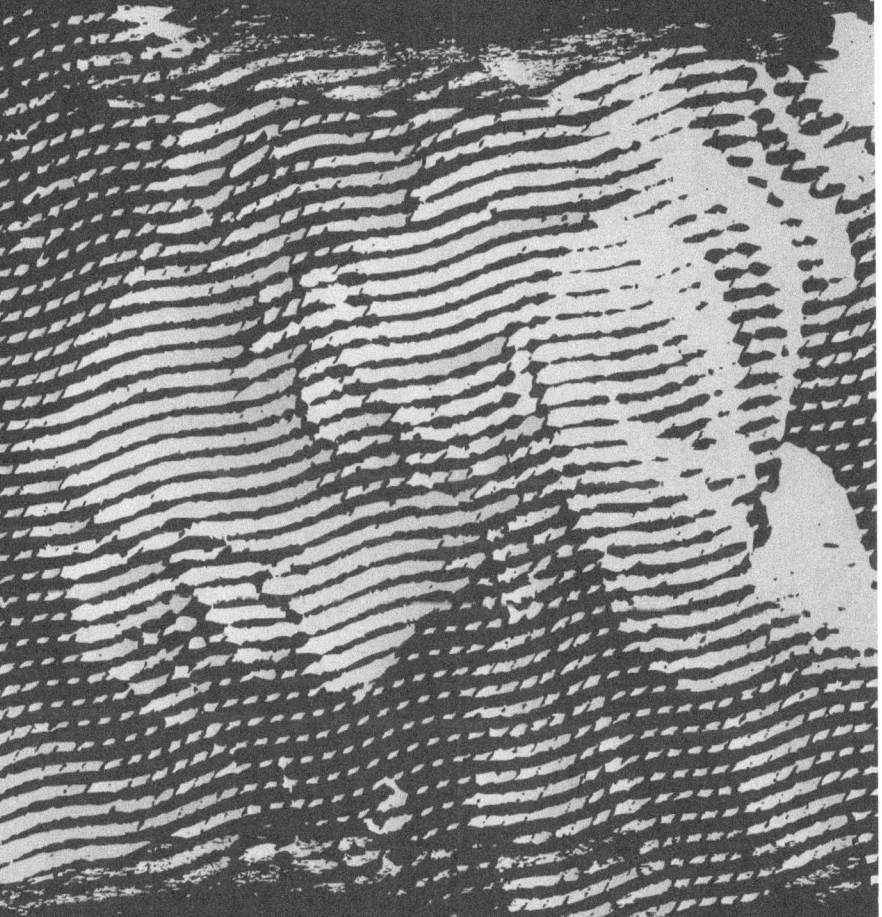

Separation

Kevin Boileau

also by Kevin Boileau

Literary

A Reason and A Season

The Patient

The Blue Pearl

Abject Poverty

99 Deceptions

The Return

Coming Soon

The Bishop... A Fisherman

3 Rivers

Outlaw Series

Theory

Genuine Reciprocity and Group Authenticity
  First Edition

Genuine Reciprocity and Group Authenticity:
  The Social Ontology of Sartre & Foucault

The Algebra of History (*with David A. Boileau*)

Essays on Phenomenology and the Self

Manifesto on Solidarity: Ethics for a New World

Coming Soon

The Psychoanalytic Approach to Mediation

Heart-of-Fire is an imprint of
EPIS Press

The Heart-of-Fire name and logo
are trademarks of EPIS Press

Printed in the United States of America
Library of Congress
1. Psychoanalysis 2. Psychology 3. Phenomenology
4. Spirituality 5. Death 6. Separation 7. Morality

"Last Slope" reprinted by permission of EPISJournal.

Cover Design: Tia Hopkins
Author Photo: NTG
Author Seal: Adrian Balasa

ISBN 978-0-9849512-3-9

The
Separation

by
Kevin Boileau

Last Slope

Winterlust crinkled along the forest trails,
Camp robbers nuzzled close
For evening's warmth.

Late rays leaned here and there
On pine-edged crests
Where tiny springs' drops
Had run nervously
From white-tressed needles.

Soon my love would stir from sleep,
Sigh and sing again.
The cold challenge would fade away
Under soft caress
Of burdgeoning winds –
My dreams will change anew

The Most Rev. George T. Boileau, S. J.
February 22, 1965
Seattle, Washington

Part

One

There was a familiarity in the darkness though I strained to make out who it was.

It was quiet—like being home in the middle of the day, sounds outside, muffled, but none that quite penetrated. Except for the dripping water.

Ting—-. Ting—-. Ting. Then it stopped, and I heard footsteps.

It was all darkness in here, along with that muffled silence, until she shuffled in. It had been a while, a very long time, but I could tell who it was from the way she stepped down the hall. Gentle and deliberate, she approached while I lay there unmoving.

Then I heard the water come on full into a pan or a bowl. Something clicked on and a sliver of yellow light forced its way into the muffled dark. It was just enough to startle me but not enough to irritate my tired, sore eyes.

The right I kept closed, the left open just enough to enframe the darkness, the narrow slit of yellow and, in conjunction with my ears, the running water.

Then the water trickled out and ended.

I would normally have expected to hear a voice coming from the movement just on the other side of the door and the yellow pencil of light, pointing its way through the entrance. But she didn't say anything and continued with the running water, padding toward me carefully carrying a bowl, until she creaked the door open.

First the hardwood floor creaked then the door.

I would also have normally greeted whoever it was with a short "Hi there" or "Hello" but it didn't seem appropriate and I was tired again, so I continued laying myself on the floor on top of a thin mat that had been placed there.

I was thirsty. My lips were dry and my head pounded.

"Take these," she said, cramming two white tablets between the fingers and palm of my left hand. She had set the bowl down on the floor and I could hear some of the water swish over the side as she pulled my hand to my mouth and with the other poured some liquid into me to push the tablets inside. Then just as quickly she found a dry rag and wiped up the floor.

"Drink more," she said. "You need it."

"Okay," I forced out of my parched lips, too tired to be anything but willing.

She wiped my face clean all the way back behind my ears and then forced another drink into me. "Rest," she said and then left.

The narrow yellow glimmer receded into nothingness as the door closed and she left down the hall. I could hear her dump it down the drain—it had been cool and welcome—until it was gone. After a few moments of wiping, I heard another light go out and I was completely in the dark.

She had put a blanket over my body—I was now in a fetal position—and a pillow under the right side of my head, so I was comfortable in my fatigue and the darkness, and was, therefore, able to drift off to sleep.

For a moment I tried to organize my thoughts into a series of questions about why I was there, but I was so tired that I lost the calculation, and danced my way into dialectic with the pitch black, silent room. There might have been a radio playing somewhere, or a light hum in the building but I couldn't tell if it was real or just in my head.

Darkness came and the analgesics must have taken hold because the pain had noticeably receded.

In conjunction with the warmth of the blanket I became a cocoon of sorts, safe in the dark quiet, with a hum in the background and perhaps a radio playing off in the distance. Like I said, it was unclear whether the sounds were from somewhere else, or just from my head.

~~~

Death was here again. It had creeped up on me in my forties when I had been a bigshot in a company and didn't have time to consider it. It had slunk around until I felt the pain and went through the tests and the treatments as fast as possible. Then I ignored it as I conquered new challenges.

But I got sick again, and had been wrestling with Death for nearly two decades. I'd been in and out of hospitals and clinics all over and had not been able to stop it. From east coast to west coast and back again, I tried the best I could to prolong the clear and inevitable End.

These thoughts danced their way in and out of my consciousness throughout the dark night as I emerged in and out of awareness.

3

My lips were dry again, the thumping in my head retreated, and I was able to fashion all kinds of thoughts in the recesses of the quiet and the solitude.

Combinatory hi-jinx, compressed tension, and the pain had become my closest friends! My ontic foolishness had turned bitter in the late October of my life! Acquisitiveness a turn-about, attachment slavish.

The dark here was so dark that it wasn't dark. The quiet was so quiet that it was nothing. Thus, it was a nothingness of dark and quiet, complete masochistic stillness that was worse than Chinese water torture.

There was the darkness of the room; the darkness of the quiet; the darkness of my sleep; the darkness of my consciousness.

I contemplated my situation.

I was no longer a young man. Most of my unformed horizon had been carved out like a small recess on my forehead, from the sadisms of the interpersonal world. [I think the cancer had come from the combustions of failed attempts to escape the quietude and the dark Eros of my heretofore masochistic strategies.]

I strained in vain to make out any sound that would upright me, that would offer me the sweet, mango-like relief from the bitter, acrid saltiness of my torment. Unfortunately, the combinatorial elements of the blanket, the dark, the quiet, alongside my physical pain and the wistful memory—-

I had walked away from so much, but I was too tired to think about it now.

So I tried going through various calculations to keep my mind busy. I was doing that now. The machinations and verbal arithmetic involved the following: How did I get here? Where was I exactly? What was the current status of my condition? The woman, how could I be sure of her identity? When would I die? Was I trapped here? What would be next?

After a time with these sorts of considerations and queries, I again became tired, and rolled on my back, hands across my chest, knees up to take the strain from my lower back. I floated back and forth between well formed thoughts and fragmented experience that was clouded with pain, darkness, and quiet, as I had mentioned. But the fatigue had its way with me, and I gave up to the night.

I allowed myself to drift, as my mind would go.

I then took inventory of my physical being starting with my breath which was shallow and irregular. It reminded me of when I had been stabbed once, lying on the ground with red liquid spilling all over the asphalt. It reminded me of when I had been caught in a major blunder, caught squarely within the Public Gaze without reprieve. Seems that I had learned from childhood that the unknown future often led to catastrophe, such beliefs engendering careful guardedness and tactical development. But this was tiring, and I was tired.

I had no idea what time it was, but I recalled being brought to her in the mid-evening yesterday. I was bathed and fed some hot soup, then brought down a flight of stairs to the warm, darkened room. The sharp pains in my body along with the headache distorted my sense of time, so I had little idea of the time other than that it was probably after midnight.

I peeled the warm blanket from my sticky skin, which the air from a nearby fan dried quickly.

I liked the cool but it exacerbated the sharp pain, which roused me from the half-sleep into which I had fallen. So much time had passed since I was a young man, but from my current perspective, had come and gone with dispatch.

I was sixty-three, considered an "old man" by many, and I felt it. The pain, the fatigue, the barely-remembered regrets—a few victories, this was all I had left. Kids had left. Wives had left. Friends were all dead or gone. Couldn't work. Couldn't think.

The dreams and the hopes were gone.

I'd played out the hand a long time ago, and now the ratio of memories to imaginings had changed for good. I was a goner and I knew it. The doctors had told me several weeks ago that I was "in the process" and agreed that I should get my affairs in order.

Thus in the space of a month, I put the beach house up for sale, paid my bills, transferred funds, wrote a set of directions, and hired someone on the little island to finish up everything. Then I headed west—it had been a long time since I'd been on that particular road—until I made it back to where it had all begun.

That was last week.

There was very little talk, just a lot of hand motions and facial expressions. Then they brought me to her last night. She knew what was going on and without reticence or interrogation had set a bowl of hot soup in front of me. Then the bath and the analgesics. I could see them talking to her, speaking loudly lest she not hear, and I ended up down here.

"Get some sleep," she cackled after she left my room with the bowl of water.

It was familiar, the dark and the quiet. In the old days this had driven me to a restless, uncomfortable state of being so much so that I left young. I found a way and left. The way doesn't matter. The fact of the leaving does. Furthermore, even though I had been back there from time to time, I wasn't required to deal with the dark and the quiet, the stillness of abjection, the quietude of death—until He fell sick some years back.

I hadn't stayed long, just enough for some serious conversation and profound reckoning. Then I left back to my life in the East and felt resolved in a full, complete way. The dialectic in the Symbolic had reached a state of equilibrium for me; this allowed me the luxury of further exploration into my imaginal states—excavating, digging, uncovering.

The heat must have kicked on because I could hear a light humming coming from what must have been the core of the house where she had filled the water, where the towels were. In conjunction with the pillow and the blanket, I started to feel a fragmentary and transitory sensation of comfort.

Safety.

I realized that the "fan" had been the heat, which had now turned on as a way to combat the cold that was permeating in from outside. I welcomed it and for the first time in months started to relax. It was intermittent, cyclic with the pain in the chest, the pain in my stomach, and the grinding on my hips and knees.

What I was having a hard time with was the realization that *there wasn't going to be much more* [time?] *for me.*

With this realization came another: that what often pulled humans out of their depression and their misery was the ongoing possibility of *something more* coming along. The first inklings of this insight had come somewhere in my 40s when I realized the simple mathematical proportion of life lived in relation to its balance. Perhaps most poignantly, this ratio shifted constantly and never to the good, unless one interpreted Death as good. Otherwise, it was exactly like slipping down a ravine while frantically pulling at roots and shrubs to stave off the inevitable.

Somehow I'd gone from thirty to sixty in the blink of an eye and I was still trying to figure out who I was, still trying to understand the early separation—something I had not been ready for and from which I had still not recovered. I'd gone through the usual resisting and defending that most men do as a way to perfect their individuation, but was still feeling the reverberations from my initial weaning, and I still wanted nothing of it. Now I was sick, feeble, and had given up my hopes for anything Good let alone anything at all.

It was an un-consolable sadness, with the *knowledge that there wasn't going to be much else for me.* This is the part that was becoming even more difficult than the early separation from her.

How was I going to live out the remainder knowing how slight it was?

How could I gain any sense of ease that would transcend my growing discomfort regarding both my physical pain and my existential suffering?

As I drifted in and out of consciousness deep in the night's belly, full of pain, tormented by my questions, I fought sleep. I think this was due to the innate capacity humans have to control their environment, or at least have some influence. It is perhaps that we come alive—emerge into consciousness and being—by saying "No" in some way, no matter what the circumstance. Now add my situation to this tendency and one can see how much I wanted to, and needed to, exercise my will dead into the dark and the emptiness.

Eventually I gave in to my exhaustion, as I said, and allowed my awareness to dissipate into the nothingness surrounding me.

There were no shadows.

It was so black in here that there wasn't even a stage for dreaming. There was no light and therefore no contrast, and everything just melded together: my hands 'cross my chest, my breath shallow and fitful, the hum and the air, no yellow from the door, the throbbing from my midsection, the anticipation of less, and the black quiet. I got myself into such a state that I lost track of time and teetered on the verge of not caring whether I would ever wake up. Sleep came on—

~~~

Warm and fluid, the lights and then the voices came. I could feel the dog's hair against my neck, nestled fully against me his weight. The sun had receded from the yellow kitchen for a while, having become tired, television still a troubadour from earlier—relentless. Phone calls and walks outside. Events with others like us, and the train tracks pulling, always suggesting, and then the light turned dark. He would come home.

There was a tension in the air; it was between them, and I could feel her being pulled away from our intimacy of the day. Then he would raise his voice and they would argue. I could hear clashing sounds—cacophonic—out in the kitchen while we would huddle down into the blankets in the semi-dark. Then the shouting would stop and he would come out with a smile. We'd smell the dinner and he would be friendly—play with us—wrestle around—bark at the dog—paw at us a bit so we'd think he was interested, but we could smell the fatigue and frustration like we could smell what she was cooking, and we'd silently be on our best behavior.

There were those proto-looks of knowing, the mutual acknowledgement of our plight and the fear response that would make us bear down; still, there was love, that mutual regard that family members have for each other even if they cannot stand one another. And it was there, lingering in the air as we were encouraged into there, to where the cacophony had been, where the smells were coming from.

Then we'd eat together and there were smiles and good feelings. Everyone would relax until we were all full. Then he would leave to clean up and take a short walk out into the evening air: cold in the winter, fresh in the summer; fall and spring in between and unpredictable. The dishes would vanish from the table, into the bathroom we went: teeth brushed and faces cleaned, changed into bedtime clothes, and back to the couch for just a bit more of the television. He'd be back by then, and we'd be ushered off to bed with kisses and hugs by both—more warm feelings and family spirit.

They were good times!

Then the darkness would come, it came upon me fast as I could hear the muffled voices out front—out there, and they were not so cacophonic, muted while the television played itself out and the black came. Tired.

Yellow, crisp morning hit as the blades of new sun tore through the windows and struck everywhere until they got to the back where we were still huddled. Warm and dark, we were still ensconced in the safety of the backroom long after he had left again for the morning shift, until she splashed the cold water on us for cleaning. Then into the yellow kitchen we went—ate—played inside, played outside, hugging the ephemeral moments of our innocence until he came home again, and the cycle would repeat.

Well, it repeated until the weekend and he would sleep for two days straight. Then we would all be quiet, taking our cues carefully, until the new week would come.

Occasionally, there would be others, and some of them would crawl on the floor and all over the furniture-our turf-and we were always glad when they left. The dog would nudge them out, my parents would start the cacophony, and we'd end up in the back room in the dark, out of earshot as much as thin walls could afford. Then the darkness would creep in dotted with waves of interruption until it was all over. Then she'd come in like always, and fuss until the quiet came too. Fait accompli!

Fetal position.

Unmoving, so still that nothing could penetrate the solidity. The air a protective sheath until it became unbearable and the coldness would penetrate into the family's transient moments of mutuality. I fought to keep that solidity of quiet, dark, and warmth—contained on both sides by her fussing moments and the cold water of daylight and cleanliness.

I felt it now, that solidity, which was interrupted only by the throbbing or the aching from my midsection and my anticipation of the cold-water blades of morning. At the same time, I both hoped for and dreaded her most likely movements of the morning.

The blackness and the quietude was unnerving—that sort of energy in a semi-tropical and humid environment in which the unmoving air encircles you like a tomb until you are ready to tear a wall down, knife your neighbor, or shoot the first man who fucks with you.

It was that still energy that was entombing me now except

for the anticipation of her in the morning and the humming sound of the air blower, which blew just enough air on my exposed left shoulder to keep my treacherous, destructive thoughts at bay. It was the pain, too, which had grown steadily worse over the years, especially the past several months that mixed with that air as an exit from the torment of the stillness.

At one point the air and the pain coincided in just the right ratio to drive me into an inescapable awake state, so I tightened my hands cross my chest and lay there unmoving—an eternity of moments one right after the other—waiting for what came next. Several minutes into this anticipation, I had the opportunity to retreat from it enough to appreciate that in my tired, pained, strained state, I was afforded a human's honor of knowing that there was *something more coming, a nascent future emerging, at least in this moment.* Its length was irrelevant in this dark succession of instants because I was able to adequately pretend that the "Now" moment was all and everything which I learned was another illusion.

We coveted the future, we humans, and traded it like precious stones. We'd cut each other's heart out for it sometimes, for its high value. With this realization at the forefront of my awareness, I am certain that a smile broke from my cracked and torn lips—another pain, but a joy as well.

Then I lost track of the succession of instants, the humming, the throbbing, and the enjoyment of the future.

It was so delicious, my immediate future, into the night, knowing that the cold water of the morning would ratify my present. There was no ticking of a clock, but in my imagination I could plainly hear the "ting, ting" of the dripping water from last night, and relished its return. Again, I fought the intrusion of alien ideas that tried to force their way into the Door of my consciousness, the feelings I had in response, narrowing my attention on the pure enjoyment of that interstitial corridor from one moment to the next, from what I reified as the present moment as it died and decayed into the next, and the next, and the next.

Then, I heard a noise. It was running water.

I lifted my head just a fraction of an inch to tilt my ear toward the direction of it, straining myself without actually moving or changing position, maintaining the relative purity of the warm cocoon into which I had drawn myself, fetal and all.

It was the solidity of the moment that had enveloped me; it was the *massif* solidity that I had craved my whole life, especially during my immersion into the symbolic and a tortured relationship with Him—which was now settled.

For just a second my thoughts diverted from the pain as I rubbed my upper lips across my parched, rough lowers. I was dehydrated again, which consistently raised my sensitivity to the pain emanating from my core. The rubbing drew me out of the centralized pain enough to desire whatever it was on the other side of the pitch-black room. I'd had enough of the solidity for now even though it offered me reprieve from the grinding, aching relentless of my eventual demise. The rubbing awakened me to the running water sound and my imagination of the water bowl from last night. Then I heard a knock at the door as she entered.

"It is morning," she said, entering. "It is early."

Then she walked over to me with the bowl, her steps illuminated from the yellow light that penetrated into the darkness just like before. She set it down, and went to light a candle, whose flame started its dance immediately while she washed my hands and face with a rag full of warm water.

"Later, you will take a bath. For now try to sit up. I will bring you some tea, then a bit of soup. You were so weak—almost dead—when they brought you to me. We need to get you strong."

Strong? What was the point in being strong if I were ineluctably being thrown off the cliff to an unknown end? I had always thought that weakness could eventually end in the lowest possible wattage, before the light went out.

I was too tired to respond other than with a feeble "Okay," trying hard to prop myself up against the pillows that she'd recovered from a closet in the room.

I was so tired and weak that my arms shook as I struggled to get my face off the sleeping mat but after some effort, I was able to sit.

I was compliant and offered her my arms, first one then the other, so she could wash me further. After she'd gotten most of the sweat, she wiped my face a final time and left the room through the yellow sliver that came from the hall. She came back with hot tea and I drank all of it almost too quickly—it soothed the lips and temporarily suppressed the pain in my stomach area.

A little while later she came with soup, a bowl of it that she had placed on a wooden serving tray that she pushed up against me.

"Eat all of it," she said. "It's good for you."

Spoon after spoon I slurped it into my cracked lips and pained body. I'd eaten this kind before, many years ago, the present smell and taste causing a flood of memories into my consciousness. Since then—from the early times—I'd gotten her soup propitiously, in ways that helped me crack one of the codes of life or provide me with temporary shelter.

It had been a long time—a very long time—since I'd had the soup.

After I'd left home it was perhaps yearly that I would visit, but at one point I had to go away on a long journey which took me far, far off the main track of my history; as such, my visits became letters. These became memories eventually. This was well before my resolution with Him; in fact it was this long journey that had precipitated such uproar.

I learned rather quickly in my youth about his disdain and disapprobation for my choices in the symbolic—my interpretational choices along the winding path. Because there was no room for dialogue—let alone dialectic—I was pushed into an alienated position, askew to new experience and linguistic relation. Before then, it was just an oscillation between the solidity and the coldness, vulnerable to the capriciousness of her unconscious and the frail tenuousness of their union.

But during the weekdays we were alone, until my brother came along. Until then, there was a density, a thickness in my experience that involved a lifelong clash between the natural rhythms of my life and the principled offerings that she made in accord with what she thought she ought to do.

It was the soup that operated as salve in this dissonance, or the rag with the warm water, both emerging within the yellow paint of the kitchen and the sun that sometimes was able to angle its way in to our home. His after-work arrivals and the occasional guests that we received were mostly just interruptions in that solidity, so naturally I felt out of sorts when they happened.

Yet here she was with the soup and the warm water,

ministering to my pain and the interrupted-ness of my life that had grown beyond fathomable proportions.

They'd had to scoop me back from disaster—nearly fatal—and then didn't know what to do with me until someone suggested that she was still alive. Then they tracked her down, and were glad to ship me off to her. And now I was here in the dark, sitting, enjoying the immediate memory of the soup, intermixed with the pain—and the darkness broken from her appearance.

I was warm, and I enjoyed the solid hand of darkness that enveloped the room, broken only by her footsteps and the yellow light.

The soup and the tea and her voice were further aspects of it—the solidity, which I welcomed as counterpoint to the pain. But then the pain became the solidity, broken only by the light and water, and the exchange of words.

I feared that there was nothing left except this withering weakness, pain, and decay and yet was intrigued by her new presencing in my life. Curiously, it created an anticipatory feeling that left me wondering what would happen next, what she would do. This was interspersed with my belief that my end was near, the pain that I could count on.

The morning had broken now even though I could not see the sun.

It had broken through the sweat of the night and the stiffness of my limbs. It had pierced the glove that had wrapped itself round my soul, squeezing me into nothingness.

Then she came with the water; she came with the rag and the bowl and cleaned me. She said to rest for a bit and then would help me into the bath just on the other side of the yellow.

Everything hurt as she helped me up and into the warm liquid, which was imbued with steam that hid my flesh, water that cleansed my shame and resignation. We didn't speak, hadn't spoken other than her gentle commands.

She pointed out a glass of cold water on the edge of the bathtub, saying to "drink all of it. I'll check on you in a short while." Then I hobbled and inched myself across the floor into the steam, being careful to leave my diseased, smelly rags outside the door, "to be thrown away."

It was all I could do to not spill the water she had poured for me, sitting on the lip of tub. I used the remaining strength that was in my shoulders and arms to angle myself across the edge of the tub and into the water. Then I lost my grip and fell the rest of the way into it, which covered all of me—my eyes and my face; I let go, for I had no more resistance. I let it wash over my pain and allowed myself not to think about anything. I arranged myself on my back so that my hands were crossed over my chest just under the water line.

Unfortunately, I felt the constraint of the pain when I stopped moving. In response, when I moved to avoid this pain, I pushed myself out of the solidity—the repose that I craved. I wanted the repose. Thus I went back and forth between the painful but so needed solidity and the relief of the movement that carried the loss of repose. This was my reduction.

At one precious point in the interstitial corridor between this oscillation, I experienced a timeless that I had never known before except once just before he left. It—the timelessness—broke through the nihilations—the nothingness between people, between her and me.

Just before she came in again I experienced it again crossing the bridge between the pain and solidity. This transported me to that moment, one eye meeting the fire of the sun and the other trained on his body as he jumped into the river on his way back home.

I turned both away from and into the tensive admixture of my view of the river and the riveting sun. Nearly paralyzed physically, I was able to receive and to experience the most amazing imaginatory vision I'd ever had. He was gone, that was certain and so I backtracked to the dirt road which would take me forward, and I walked. It was hot and my body full of sweat; sagebrush and blue. A hawk flew overhead. And so I walked.

Then I was alone and the hawk, gone. I was all men and all people walking. I was on the path walking. On the road of my choices and my destiny, together, walking into my future— always forward. Crying with joy and sadness, I cried. And I continued walking, knowing it was time—again, it was.

Time.

There was no one in front of me; no one behind. My heart was body light and heavy, tired with anticipation. So I talked.

I talked to myself: I have hated you and I have loved you. Now I am just grateful. Sad that we must part, but beyond generous with joy that you have carried me this far on this long path. I can feel you leaving me, knowing what I must do today, at this time.

Filled with grief, ready to fly ahead, and sick with sorrow that you won't be coming with me. I am talking to you—Myself— seeing you die in front of me; it's happened over a long time, several years, but I can see your age, your fragility, your need to rest for all time. Closer to me than my mother, my father, my brother, and my sister, or any of my friends—some gone, some here.

I felt you cry against the skin of my neck, breathing into my ear: You can. You have been waiting your whole life for this

*parting. You can. You will. And I will always weep with joy
at our journey. And further: we were always here; always in
the end even in the beginning, we just didn't see it. But it was
always here, this parting. And we will be closer together than
we ever have been, and always were, as you step forward and
leave me. Our spiritual memory will be enough.*

*I slowed down then, in the road, and then stopped when
I knew it was time. My eyes no longer my own; watching
me with love and gratitude as the outlines of spirit started
protruding from my body, separating from me. Old. Wiser. So
tired and in need of the eternal rest that would bring him to
me in the netherworld at some other place and at some other
time beyond Time.*

*He looked at me and I at him, in our parting closer than we
had ever been. There was so much I wanted to say but there
was no need: he had heard it all from me before and would
forever—the sounds of my voice ricocheting off the cliffs and
rocky crags forever. And here we were out in the desert alone,
free from all the turmoil and distractions of the others. Time
slowed as I slowed—as my heart filled with such gratitude
and joy and sadness.*

*"Now," he said. "It is time." And he looked at me with such
timeless—it was me looking. And I saw him looking at me,
saying "Please. I am so tired. You must go on without me or
you will die. There is much ahead for you." Such conviction
and such joy came with the look, his regard, my regard for me,
myself.*

~ His spirit protruding.

*I wiped the sweat and my tears from my forehead. I placed my
arm around his back, my hand cupped to hold him gently, as
he further pulled away into the dry clean air. Our eyes locked.
They were open to let everything in and to pass through him.
Everything passed between us.*

~ Through us, from this hot ground into the relieving sky.

The scission grew more, greater. Our aloneness became more pronounced. I was aware of the separating, could see if clearly, but I had never felt so whole, so solid within myself. With what little strength he had left, I could feel him pushing against me to complete the process. To complete the me that we had become. Coming right out of my soul into the air, my arm and hand cupped around him to lay him down onto the road gently. Further down, into the air, and closer to the pavement, next to the salty dirt.

I lay him down, our eyes solid with mutual regard. Looking. Looking at. Looking together. He stopped talking. I could see that he was not going to say anything more to me and I died a thousand times in that moment because I wanted the words. I needed the words.

But he was looking at me, deep into me. Into us he looked, as his tired body touched the scorched earth, touching one layer of cells and then more, as the weight of his brittle self sank deep into oblivion, my hands and arms holding him—our gaze locked into eternity.

~ Only my hands kept us together now.

He became lighter in my arms, as light as the light wind in late summer in the mountain country. Light as the light white clouds billowed overhead to warn of coming rain. Light as my heart was one day before they took the light from me. Light as light. And rain. Except that now it was hot and alone as he allowed himself to press further into the earth, the body nearly lifeless.

I could hardly breathe in this passing; in this passage I was left in the solidity of the heat and heavy light, the sun drawing me forth and I fought movement. The solidity had protected me, carried me thus far, and I was terrified and exhilarated both by this road that receded in front of me, into nothingness. Our eyes still locked in love and kindness and I felt at once my own father and my son—I was both in this moment.

The wind kicked up into my face with a lightness I had not known since I had become. The wind stirred up in my soul lighting the embers as his lifelessness allowed me—no, forced me to, to withdraw my hands and then arms from him. He lay there. I watched, breathed. The sharpness of his profile, the contours of his shape started to soften, and to erode, his eyes still fixed—no, transfixed—on me, inculcating in that instant the blueprint of love for all time past [healed], into the uncertainty forward, and eternally in this moment that we share.

A hawk flew overhead and waited. There would be others.

~ His body now a shell, lifeless.

His eyes were wide so that all of eternity would enter and pass through, Him. His eyes so wide that I went in there with him, and together we shared a lingering retrospective of all that had passed. All the anguish, the suffering, the confusion: the pain withdrew into that burning land, his eyes refusing to close as I straightened up. I completely withdrew myself from the lifeless husk and looked into the sky: the hawk had disappeared. Salty wet dripped from my eyelid shutters, open to the light.

For one moment—and it was only one moment—I hesitated. I had drawn myself tall, into my fully erect standing position looking down at him. At me. (I seemed smaller then, which was a curious fact that I still pondered years later.)

I was being pulled forward on the road out into the distance so I looked for another moment deep into his eyes, no longer eyes but portals into everything. Then I turned around with tears streaming down my face, admixtures of everything that I had been and all that anyone could ever be. Faced with the reality of my lifeless past and an unknown future, his sweat mine, and my heart his forevermore, I walked forward on this road.

~ One step then the next I walked.

It couldn't have been more than a few, perhaps ten or so, then I stopped and turned around. I could see there, the lifeless form—it was me—what I had been from the beginning of time, what I will already be when I am there again in this rotating dream. I looked around and saw him—no, me—sunk into the ground and during that space of the ten steps he had reached out his hand to me.

The body was now deeply sunken into the ground—dead— but the hand was reached out to me, open and grasping in unison with his eyes trained carefully on me as I drew into the future. With unknown strength and love the hand was outstretched to me, the arm drawn its full length, the eyes open pools of gratitude. It was the hand of love that had opened to me that caused me such joy. He had given absolutely everything to me to get me here, to this point. He had given everything for me.

Even in the dry burning heat, the sticky tears dripped down from my eyes. I continued looking at his open hand and without intention I raised mine to him. As I raised my hand, looking, holding my arm and my hand outstretched, joining, across that nothingness, his eyes—my eyes—started to close. And his hand fell to the ground. As his hand fell to the ground, my eyes closed from the heat and the dizziness and the gratitude.

Then I heard another voice calling from an unknown place in the dark, across the yellow of the sun—

~~~

In one moment He had jumped into the river and her voice woke me. "Are you all right in there? Can you get out of there by yourself?"

I pulled my hands from across my chest and positioned them on the bottom of the tub so I could raise myself up. She was on the other side of the door.

"I know it hurts," she said. "After you are done, would you like to sit in the courtyard? It's sunny and warm there."

She was asking, I noticed, which I welcomed from her—the asking. Even though it had been many years—the memories of her principled methods of love and care had burned a hole in me, a whole me. As such, I had set out to mediate the distance between desire and principle in the world of men—the symbolic.

"Yeah, " I said. "Give me a few minutes. I think I can get up."

"Okay," she replied. "I'll just sit out here. Let me know if I can help."

An honest, mutual exchange was what this was, and even I could recognize it even though it was everything I could do to push myself into a sitting position in the hot, murky water.

I tried unsuccessfully at first to raise myself out of the water but couldn't. The last several months dealing with my illness had weakened me to such an extent that I couldn't get up, so I allowed myself to sink back into the soapy, murky tub.

I knew she was out there and would come in to help if I asked, but I refrained. I wanted her to help but I refrained. I wanted her to come in and help me out of the water and into the robe she had laid out for me. But it had never been that way for us. Instead, it had been resistance and counter between principle and need, rule and desire, always a nothingness separating us.

The gulf had been unbearable for most of my life until I thought my way through it, but I believe that this sort of hand-clenching and problem-solving was responsible for the disease that would soon end my life.

"I can make it," I said, hearing her shift around a bit in the chair.

I was so tired. Hot. Pain ripping through my core and into my joints but the warmth of the water was welcoming. Withdrawing from it hurt more, at a different level, as I left the solidity of it—feeling the colder air against my skin.

I had angled myself against the lip of the tub and was able to huddle against it and eventually fell over it and onto the floor, wet, colder, but there. I crawled to the towel and then to the robe. I wrapped them both around me as best I could and then fell onto the floor in a heap.

"Are you okay?" she asked.

"Yes, just give me a minute. I'll be out in a minute."

Then I passed out on the floor.

Some time later, I felt her there with me getting me into the robe and handing me water. Such joy I felt in her care—non-principled and responsive, pulling me out of the solidity in such a way that I welcomed it. This happened without my preparation or foresight, this experience of being pulled out, by choice or otherwise, from the solidities that we seek in order to re-create that initial vacuum of the watery womb. As an aside, I realized that this change did not need to be some big dramatic event heralded and presaged with, but the change was delightfully surprising—and welcomed.

It's not that the behavior was different; it was actually similar to what I remember, but there was a different tone and sense to it, almost ineffable, but it offered me a new sort of relief from my fatigue and the pain.

It took a while to get me up the stairs. In fact it took nearly an hour from the time I woke up on the bathroom until I made it to the courtyard where she helped me situate myself in a chair on the tile next to the pool, the sun out— skies clear.

And it went like this for some time: We would go to the bath, to the courtyard, to the kitchen. Then I'd fall asleep on the couch watching movies or trying to re-read some of the German philosophy I hadn't tried hard enough at when I was younger.

~ *And his eyes closed, outstretched hand falling to the ground, and with that the Door closed, ending that heretofore, unresolved incident in the playground of my past. And the hawk reappeared soaring with judiciousness—aiming.*

The wrenching from inside my gut came on stronger. It would usually start in the early morning but would subside after the oatmeal. It would go away—latent but gone—that is, until lunchtime when I wouldn't be hungry, but she would encourage me to eat:

"For your strength," she said. In the afternoon, she would bring licorice tea and analgesics; by then I was hurting again, and the throbbing wouldn't completely recede as the evening came on. This cycle just got worse, as my sickness took over and crushed me into the abjectivity of blood, joints that barely worked, brittle bones, rancid breath— creeping solidity that unfortunately had partnered with

Pain.

I developed a fever, too, so I wasn't too clear-headed anymore. Yet this helped me up and down the stairs, from the dark—to the bath—to the courtyard—to the living room in the afternoon when she would go out for groceries and come back to make dinner. It was during this time that I would alternate between watching images on the television, listening to the music that was always on, regulating myself with more narcotics as needed, and on occasion I would saturate myself with silence.

This was a full silence that fulfilled my desire for solidity. It was the pure-white snowfield untainted—motionless. It was the cerulean I'd seen off the coast of Spain. The perfect ratio of shoulder to hips. Two in the morning on the mall in that college town. A certain smile. Riding the metro in the east, watching the city go back until I was in the country, alone. That beer. That tea: knock, knock! Clunk.

She was home again. She would be home and the visions and memories of these solidities would transform into stark, abject pain. Even the dinner wouldn't help, but she would help me—without it I would have been gone sooner.

Even so, I could feel it slipping away while she was ministering to me. I was weaker each day, and sometimes the light hurt so I would spend more time downstairs in the dark room, which gave me some relief. The fever didn't ever completely break, though, and my thoughts became incomplete and fragmented.

I remember she would look at me that way and the sun would fill the kitchen, mixing with the yellow walls until it was a golden admixture of "being here." Watching my smile in the mirror, food on my chin, the steady sound of baby being milked created such splendor.

One morning she had to carry me to the bathroom; it was more like dragging, but I couldn't move I was so groggy from the narcotics and pain, intermixed into a smelly pit of negation. It was hard for her to get me in there because she was so old—wizened—but with the help of an old wheelchair we could angle me directly into the bath.

It was a harmonious, cooperative enterprise: the old woman and the sick, dying man. The situation had its parameters and roles and both of us played them well, listening here and negotiating there.

One day while sitting in the courtyard—it was sunny and warm with just a light breeze—I was able to discern the gap between her former principled approach and the practical mutuality in which we were now engaged. Perhaps this was because we realized that time was running out; perhaps it was due to eroding memories of the primal scene—the original polis was long deceased. It was now just two, and when I left, she would be alone in her own solidity. Thus, reparations were for both.

One day—I don't remember the day of the week or month, although I suspected it was spring because the snow had recently thawed out—it was harder than normal to get me up and out of the darkness. The throbbing was in my stomach and my head, both at the same time, and the rhythm of my heart was irregular. She tried to get me up but I was too weak, so she let me collapse on the mat in the dark. I stayed there all day I think until she brought me some soup, which I ate by yellow candlelight.

She'd come in periodically, I could tell when the yellow light came into the room, to check on me.

"How are you feeling?" she'd ask. Or she'd say, "It's a beautiful day, sun's out."

But she did not push and did not pry. She allowed me my illness, which for me, was the greatest of generosities. "It really hurts," she questioned. I could only nod or mumble assent—but the gift was tangible, in stark contrast to the original pronouncements about getting tough, and so forth. Here, I could just be weak and sick. It was the greatest of gifts!

After spending the day in the dark—knowing that my time was drawing near—I was able to drag myself up to the kitchen with her help. Dinner was soup and lean meat. I felt the hot tea warming into the evil that would soon take me. And during the evening, the sun waning, the narcotics fighting off the pain—losing the battle—I was able to begin a spiritual transformation as well. She started it by asking about death. She talked about Him.

We talked about his passing and the preparation he had made for "the journey," as she called it. This intrigued me greatly and whatever clarity I had that escaped the immolation of my consciousness.

"Your father, just weeks before he left us, started talking differently—about returning. I figured it was due to the pain, or to the church."

She leaned in to me, by now the sun gone, and she spoke in quite tones.

"It was like a different voice took over, one that I'd only gotten fragments of in our life together. It was from a different place." I was by now propped up in the couch, listening intently but struggling to hear. To be here.

She dimmed the lights and lit more candles. I sunk into the fabric. She drank a small glass of red, and continued to talk about Him. I was by now in a half sleep of narcotic, pain, and fatigue, and she was nothing more than a dream figure.

Complete thoughts were becoming more difficult to muster but hoped that the overall sense was something I could apprehend. It was like losing my hearing, my sight, and my smell all at once. I was drowning.

And it went on like this into the night. She offered me more tea and more water, and the candles burned down, casting shadows on the walls. This was the same house I had grown up in; the same house I had suffered the nothingness that separates; the place where need and principle diverged:

He spoke of returning—quite often in the end. There was a look about him, beyond the grief of dying; beyond the separating from love; beyond pain. He was somewhere else during these looks, which I had first noticed early on in our life together but which became more pronounced as I became more aware of them. I'd notice it when we were driving in the mountains and he'd stop to take in the expanse. But I realized it was not the expanse he was taking in; instead, he was building final memory to take with him. I didn't know how this could be true but it became obvious to me.

I wonder if you've had these thoughts, too.

I fought so hard to stay awake while she spoke. I had transcended the pain and the grief, but wasn't quite sure what she was saying. The words got jumbled around in my head and went something like this:

Your father, he has been preparing to return—no need to be sad at the funeral.

But this didn't make any sense to me. We'd already been to his funeral: I remember looking across the wooded slope of green grass and oak, outside of the burial, and I thought I saw him there looking at us. But this didn't make any sense. He was dead. And it was still true that I saw him looking— both away and toward us.

Still on the couch, wasn't sure if we'd been outside or downstairs. It seemed that the candles hadn't burned down, same scene, same shadows. Her soft voice murmuring, pitter-patter sequences of sounds that no longer had meaning yet the tempo and the inflection were comforting. I refused the narcotics now, preferring the pain and the fatigue and what awareness I had left.

Twilight. Morning. The spaces in between. The interstitial corridor. Flickering fragments of awareness intertwined— no caught—like the sharp catches the fabric and unwinds it. Candlelight.

Memories of him in that green-lawned cemetery looking at us with gratitude and at the long journey home ahead—wistful of the leaving, wistful of the return; and now I realized why I'd never "known" him. He, himself, was unaware of the deeper artery though he'd been generously given enjoyable glimpses throughout his sojourn here on this land.

What was it to be my forefather? What was the job? Why hadn't I known about all this from the beginning?

I remember him walking away from the green lawn as the sayings were said and the weeping pronounced. I managed to slip away and follow him all afternoon until he made it to the river. He turned around and acknowledged me, told me he'd known I would follow, that I—alone—would watch his departure. And the sun was hot; shined in my eye. Salty tears on my cheeks. Joy, intrigue, sadness. Why couldn't I follow? Why had he to go?

"You will understand all of this one day—at the Gathering. You will know what to do. Go back now. Go back. You must not follow me. I left, mumbling to Him.

"Shush—[she rubbed my shoulder]. It's okay. You were dreaming."

She was wiping sweat from my face. Shadows and candlelight crisscrossed on the wall. She told me it was late, that everything would be okay soon. I sunk deeper into the fever and stopped caring about what time of day it was anymore. She continued moving me from the dark into the light and back, between the hot and the cool, but it was all a blur by now. The pain-free moments were fleeting but it was hard to distinguish them anymore because I was so tired and feverish.

It became difficult to keep my eyes open.

She lit more candles and kept the lights off.

We stopped taking me downstairs because it was too hard to get back up. She made me eat soup once or twice a day, but it didn't matter. On occasion she'd drag me out to the courtyard during the late afternoon when it had started to cool.

She'd started telling me stories about the old days when I was little, which put somewhat of a smile on my face. She told me stories about her life before then—when she was a little girl—and stories about her grandfather that she'd heard. But the words made little sense to me; it was the tone and the feeling that I followed, which was pleasant. Otherwise, I just lay here, on the couch, sometimes on the floor with a blanket and a pillow.

It grew darker and my fever never broke, and I enjoyed watching the flames from the fireplace; they danced and fed me, and allowed me to walk into my imagination. Darker. Quietude. Gentle. Reversing course on a trail I'd already been on. I nestled into the warmth of the fire and the blanket, and my fever.

Part

Two

They found me in the alley behind "Stingers," one of the beach community's best dive bars. Someone had smacked me on the back of the head and taken my wallet, so they had to sit with me until I was coherent enough to tell them who I was. From the type of suit I was wearing, they figured out I was a local professional who'd been in the wrong place at the wrong time.

Then I came to, saying "I'd just stopped off on the way home at the framing shop next door."

Everything after that was a blur. Later that day they found my wallet. After more questioning they discovered that perhaps I'd had a couple of drinks in the bar while I was waiting for the painting to be framed.

"You don't look well," one of the officers said, noticing my pain as I clutched my midsection.

He reached out, thinking that maybe one of my ribs had been broken in the assault, but I assured him it was a longstanding pain for which I was being treated at the local hospital. After all the administrative part of the ordeal, they let me go home. I was out $50 cash and a dirty suit but otherwise unscathed.

"Take care of yourself," another said, with just a hint of paternalism, which caused me to take a long hard look in the mirror before I got into my car and left.

It was the lifelong scission that got to me.

It was some point early on that they announced that I had to go to "kindygarden," to which I had no choice but to assent. Then I started first grade; that's when they taught me from the books that we were supposed to learn. The problem was that I wasn't ready to leave the good deal I had going at home with Her. I was encouraged and persuaded then eventually forced, and I ended up in a large room with a large number of kids.

It was hell. This was the beginning.

There were all these formulas we had to learn. Rules. Protocols. Later, my job at the grocery store wasn't too bad once you learned the way things were supposed to go, who was in charge, what the economies of exchange were. I hated the tie—which was the first of many—and the not the last of those I reviled. This was followed by new rules with each transition.

There was baseball, and other subsidiary sports, including football, basketball, and boxing; skiing, tennis, and wrestling.

My first jobs, including the one at the grocery, were other entries into the symbolic, where I learned what counted as true and false, as well as good and bad. There were interweaving logics that permeated all daily life but which changed without prediction. There were the etiquettes and ways of society, family, school, and I was forced to learn them as I grew in consciousness. This was after they'd effectively separated me from her—which, at the time, brought me sweet relief: for I hadn't mastered the connection anyway.

Years later, I had found my place in the matrices of knowledge and power in such a way that I was able to construct a good living and an affluent situation. I became a "professional," with a nice income, new car, new house, new clothes, and regular "vacations." I was "established," as one of the friends of the family would say.

I had locked myself into the system by the time was thirty— with debt, a great job, and a promising career: I was highly promotable.

I'd left home early—in my teens—having given up on any reconciliation or resolution to the problems I'd been having with them. This is not to say that this was or is out of the norm for any young man, but it felt big, and leaving was significant. I'd also come back in a few years, when he told me how to get a well-paying summer job, which I took—and lost—because I hadn't figured out how to be "responsible."

For some hard to understand reason, I was always askew to the symbolic matrix.

Perhaps this explained why I got into it with the produce aisle manager, or wasn't taken in by the 1st grade learning, with which I was not impressed. From both of these experiences I was afforded a view into my split-apart existence—like there were two, interwoven, but different. This is not to say that it was an experience of a doppelganger because it wasn't; however, it was as if that part of me who operated within the systems of language, had to carry a "deep" me. Not the archaeological self of Freud, or anything quite as sexy as Jung, but it was if a part of me was hanging on for dear life as "I" made my way forward.

And there we were, the two of us: one. I protected him like a brother, my-Self.

He protected me, too, even though he didn't have the words to say so. Thus, I spoke for him, as if he were speaking for my benefit, which is confusing to articulate, hard to see. Thus—I am moving about in my 40s and 50s, having erected some sort of provisional ontic structure over and over again, starting at 21 when I left the university for work. What was remarkable to me at that time was the zeal with which my peers committed to careers, personal identities, and structural positions. Some of these were forced by family; others by the media. Those who expressed reticence in "choosing" were regarded as morally defective in some way—"undecided," "not yet ready," or even "lazy."

We made our way forward, he and I, two parts of an inseparable though awkward whole. It was hard to say who was navigating the uncomfortable coupling. Yet I made my way, thoroughly saturated with the ideologies of my family and my hometown—but I wasn't aware of this. This was my career.

As I said, when they found me beaten and robbed in the alley, it wasn't surprising, according to my co-workers. I'd been working so hard—for years—and I needed distractions. I'd struggled unsuccessfully for years to have a relationship to Him, but there was this gap, and I often wondered how he saw me. He never said.

The Social.

I struggled for years to find my bearings with others. After the separation, my orientation toward the Other was filled with angst, anti-socialism, and overall dread. There were numerous false starts, battles, and righteous claims; romances and friendships; family; strangers; encounters; spinning wildly from the separation—I suppose—in a frenetic attempt to regain that solidity with which I started. Of this, I was unaware and unconscious.

With her, matters were awkward. She approached me with a Germanic, principled style.

Everything in its place, and a place for everything, was her motto.

The profundity of emotion had escaped her, probably at the moment of her most intense ontological rupture. As such, our involvement was perfunctory and routinized; in some ways it was a perfect example of the mechanistic worldview of the European Enlightenment. Thus, there was a gap between my being and her ministrations—it was a nothingness toward which I grasped; but because there was nothing there save a stone, cold wall, the tempo and tone with which I learned to relate was as such: principled and German, etc. and so forth.

This nothingness permeated the rest of my relationships.

Working my way backward retrospectively, I was able to trace the genealogy of my fractured pattern to its paradigm case.

"How long have you been like this?" was common.

However, with the introjected Germanic mien, I was able to internally parry the steely, knife-like commentary with my own version.

Trips to Las Vegas worked great, just like trips to the outskirts of towns, the seedy parts. My romantic interplay was orchestrated by television and other media, but this "intellectualized" approach was often met with more of the principled approach in return—which made it a farce. Still, there was a forward-moving intentional structure that promised something new just over the rise.

For example, "Katie," as she liked to be called, was more

than willing to fix our situation, ostensibly through love, but even this had its limits and proved temporally fatal. Yet, she went the extra mile, something that most people are not willing to do; for that reason, we established an eternal karmic relationship; there was nothing undone—during our time together, and long after that time had passed.

Even before then, in the early stages of becoming, the wonderment of the Other was debilitated by the stoney-cold wall, that principled approach that turned individuals into characters on a television screen. This was a relatively benign alternative to the banging of my head against that wall of alienation, and principle. After this, it became more complicated, as I had to mediate through the Symbolic—full of other people's interpretations of the "right" and the "true."

As corollary, I tried on several different career paths, one after the other, reaching for that perfect crystalline oath within myself. Unfortunately, the realities of social life chipped away from and eroded that conception, and its manifestation. I guess I just couldn't accept that any meaningful work had nothing to do with the crystalline path.

I strove for money, recognition, structure—ontological security. And though the careers changed along with the professional identities, they were all of the same logic: the true and the false, the wrong and the right, and ideological conceptions of the Good. There were strategies and tactics, and pragmatic considerations.

I was an accountant, a corporate executive, a teacher, and a host of other things—crisscrossing my way from early adulthood to when I got sick. "Foundations," they were, in my search for the crystalline, and they all ended in stylized frustrations.

Yet, my social relationships—both professional and personal—grew out of these strivings, and included attachments that kept in place my own self-concept.

In my twenties, it was competition with my peers, and pursuits of women as prizes. Work was merely a structure that fueled these adventures. In my thirties, my propensity for introspection grew, along with my abilities for instrumental reason and teleologically based friendships. "Pacts" were made, and campaigns waged—all for the feeling of accomplishment. Thus, my friendship with Oscar was solely accounted for in terms of parties and accumulated encounters or liaisons with the opposite sex.

In my other arena—"career," I made numerous other pacts with the intention to further my own self-interest, as reciprocal and mutual. It was men's play, full of the codes and competitive rules that seemed to further everyone's interests. However, in quiet moments I wondered who actually set the rules and who actually wanted them. On closer inspection, it seemed like we'd all been thrown into an alley game, and had to play well or die.

I could really see us all as separate from the "game." As separated. Separate.

However, this insight mostly served my angst——you know, the experience of staring into the abyss, asking questions, considering, becoming skeptical. Therefore, I was drawn back into the more comfortable usages of the symbolic and returned just as quickly to the languages and protocols that had been set before me. I made it from thirty to fifty in a flash, truly in the blink of any eye; by the time I caught my breath long enough to understand the bridges that I had burned, I was already halfway through the race. This led me both to the material and to the spiritual, twofold and together.

The spirit.

Even though I had abandoned the church years ago, I had come to that point that most come to when we don't have answers for the important questions. We then seek answers through religion or "spirituality" of some sort. For me, this meant making provisional any of the answers I'd come to about morality & mortality, the true and the false. I just couldn't get any bearings underneath that didn't regularly change with the seasons. But just like the realization that I was a self before I was any particular person, I came to believe that our ideologies, our claims to truth, and our choices in value—our worldviews—were all contingent constructions. Choices, as it were.

This belief allowed me the mental space to contemplate the "spiritual," those things I didn't understand or have any certainty about. And of course, this carried over into my social life because my understanding about people changed so much—like facets of a diamond—that it was quicksand too.

Nevertheless, these questions about meaning drove me obsessively, and I never stopped trying for answers.

Once I was done with solely relying on the wise men in the great books, I had no where to turn except to the spirit—the land of faith—provisional, hopeful, uncertain in a comforting sort of way. With this bracketing came the abyss though this was tinged with possibility.

Such sweet, open possibility! Something about cutting through fear with joy—the bracketing of the actual—gave me the strength to walk another step down the road of uncertainty. And another. And another again.

And I never stopped walking.

Fortunately, upon rare occasion, I was able to garner a small modicum of the great wisdoms, which provided me fuel for the great journey ahead.

Sometimes I would intellectualize the spiritual by en-framing it in the symbolic.

I would do this in an attempt to understand but I only tangled myself in the barbwire of knowledge even more. I would recognize this by the nosebleeds and my poor sleeping habits. Then, as I realized that I had been tossed back down the hill to start over, I would once again be at the intersection of thinking and being—and the spiritual.

These ruptures, however, would lead me to new paths and new motives; again, one foot in front of the other.

Everyday.

They also led me to the physical-material: the notion that there was furniture in the world and that I was a part of it.

Material.

The constant ambiguity and uncertainty in my values would strike fear in my heart and render me vulnerable to sleepless nights. This compromised my immune system, along with other destructive life patterns, and I steadily slipped into a state of illness.

It was always at my door, the illness, although I was able to keep it in the basement, at bay, enough so that no one knew. But I was acutely aware of the weakening of my body; at the same time I became more aware of the power and dangers of the physical world. In response, I tested limits as much as I could: climbed mountains, ran dangerous trails, and pushed myself against my own destruction.

At one and the same time, I both increased and decreased myself. Thus, I was an ambivalent holding pattern.

Sometimes, I would withdraw completely into myself, fully deceiving myself about my body—either that or existing in an ironic interplay with my spirit, with the nothingness that slipped through me like a ghost. This, however, would enable me greater and greater dangers in the material world, like skiing down impossible trails and holding my breath under water past the point of safety.

It was quite Germanic and principled, a steely, stone barrier against which I pressed all too often. It was here in the material-physical world that I started to learn that he was my antagonist—my dialectic.

Everything I had already felt about him I carried with me and it was He that I sparred with, always looking for successful linguistic or logical strategy in the symbolic to prove my point. I did this even after He was gone.

I continued it until I got really sick and realized what I was doing, that it was inane and fruitless. He'd owned me—and my life—and by the time I figured it out I was too late.

They said that the sickness would take me within 18 months.

When I was a young adolescent, I had little bodily awareness, and didn't make the connection between my physical being and my consciousness. I just knew that my mind was housed in my body, and that I carried it around with me. Sometimes I hurt and sometimes I felt good.

It was not until my early twenties that I came to realize that I *was* my body; more importantly, I became aware that my mind affected my body. As such, I started to see a direct correlation between my mental states and the way I felt in my body. Nevertheless, these awarenesses were all tied in to a complex relationship to Him and to the swimming sea of the symbolic.

For a long time it was not clear whether he wanted me to be like him or not.

I could not be sure what his motivations were even with the long-term questioning I put him through. Thus, my intentionality was foundationally comprised of expansion-contraction—a system of attraction/repulsion that was solely dictated by our relation.

It took a long time before I started to see Him just as a man trying to live a life; that my conception of him was not necessarily who he was; that it might be in my best interest to get some perspective about this—which I did but only after I gave myself permission to separate from the disappointments and the frustrations.

Self.

It took a while before I deconstructed the *Cogito*.

I think what precipitated my learning was the one day I was at wit's end—in trouble, serious trouble, and largely unaware of why and how these things continued to happen.

I remember the day: I was driving my car in my hometown, back for the holidays, and everything had recently gone to shit. The pastor in the church had died of cancer, unexpectedly, so I couldn't talk to him, and all my friends were worthless—even further entrenched in the muck and the slime of their facticity and the sedimentations of our township.

I stopped my car one day along the side of the road. I sat and cried, frustrated and distraught, wanting to be a "good" person, and totally freaked out that I was in trouble again—unawares of how I got there.

So I prayed.

I actually looked up into the sky, tears running down my cheeks, ignorant of my freedoms. Further, I was unaware of why I would even be making an appeal to the cosmos for salvation. Fortunately, this was the beginning of a meta-textual reflection in me for the unanswered questions. It was also the inception of fragmented insights into greater perspectives about the nature of reality.

This is not to say that I clearly or fully understood any of it.

However, the beginning of my skepticism about my own ability to perceive and to understand was liberation.

I didn't have to be sure of anything; it could all be provisional and therefore bracketed for further investigation.

When I finally got to the point where I accepted a new philosophy of mind which held that most motivation was unconscious, I actually started to relax; however, at one and the same time, the power struggle between my father's interpretations about how things were and my own was never at a higher pitch. For he held fast the belief that the important things were knowable—transparent if one would only discern them through rigorous daily practice. Instead, I chose to make everything an intellectual problem, layering such a schematic in various modulations—as my whim would dictate. However, I did come to trust the logic chains that would both get me into trouble, and out.

My self, therefore, became an interesting quagmire of both conscious hubris and painstaking skepticism, especially regarding the fragmented pieces of the early days that

It was lifelong struggle.

From one professional career to the next, seeking out the answers to the True and the Right, I edged my way forward. Tangling with Him, my father, I edged my way forward.

I don't know what I'm going to do with my life. What am I going to do?

You will be fine. Look at the wonderful opportunity right in front of you.

Yeah, but I don't know if it will change me. I don't want to change.

Well, change can be good, can't it?

No answer forthcoming. A mumbled *I suppose so.*

Later.

God, I'm glad I got the hell outta there. It was killing me.

Good experience?

What do you mean? I am almost didn't make it out.

It's just another experience. You can do anything you want with your life.

[I wonder if he knew about the burning bright light that penetrated everything.]

Or worse yet: *I want to know you. Don't you want me to know you?*

I don't know what you mean. I'm here.

Well, you never seem to let me in—you are a mystery to me. I just want to know you.

What do you want to know? I'm here.

Well, I want to understand you. You know, why you are the way you are.

What do you want to know?

This shit would cycle up over and over, and it did until I tired of it; he and I tired of it. So I would retreat, make another plan, move on, do something new. But it was always the same: my choices revolved around my conception of Him and what I believed He thought of me.

In my uncertainty, I sought strength.

With the Cogito, I sought to break it; I sought my own authenticity in my destruction. This was to retain the purity of the bright, white light that cleared the way.

After years of trying to "know" Him, I gave up, first blaming then second accepting-dejecting.

Then the dry period came.

We gave up on each other, I think, because we'd reached impasse—without breakthrough resources. Thus, I learned to fend for myself with Him in a peripheral position in the shadow areas of my consciousness.

When this point came, I realized how much in deep water I was. I'd rejected my home, my neighborhood, my church, and my family except in the most marginal of ways. Thus, I made successive attachments to new positions in the symbolic, rationalizing what didn't work as the price for what did.

The bright white light deep in the alcoves became dim—somewhat yellow and hidden.

Perhaps this was to mask the ontological terror I experienced—I don't know—but I spent several years relentlessly pursuing knowledge and understanding, with occasional Stoic-based meditations that exposed me to intuition. The bottom line here was that I kept moving—always forward.

This method of moving forward, someone said, was a well-honed, adaptive tactic that was protective.

Someone I trusted said: "moving targets are harder to hit," just before we ended our work together. In contrast, I always thought of it as teleological fuel toward one's destiny. In retrospect I saw that the white core was lighting the way even though it was dark to me at times.

I gained strength by developing my adeptness at operating within these matrices—always with an entry and exit plan, a "Plan B," and both the acumen and celerity to reconstitute myself in any situation.

I was a chameleon of sorts, a denomination that a former friend had given himself with great pride. It took me nearly 25 years from then to learn this myself.

My life became replete with stories and at one time I considered myself an experience junkie. I craved voluminous knowledge of human beings, their motivations, their dark sides, their unconscious propensities, behavioral patterns, emotions, and cognitions. I became obsessed to understand everything about the nature of our humanity.

One might ask about the lack of specific detail of my story here but I am not sure that it is too important. I believed then, and do now more so, that it was and is one's experience [interpretation, feelings, and intuitions] that is more important.

Plot just provides matches and kindling to light the flame of discovery.

However, it is also true that as I aged, I became more willing to share the interesting plot lines of the stories that fueled this reach for understanding that emerged from the white-yellow light that permeated the air space of my consciousness—poking through the wispy smoke traces that encircled me like so many hungry wolves.

I don't want to go. Can I stay with you? [flashes from first day, Kindergarten]

He's very gifted—brilliant—but we are concerned that he is so quiet. Doesn't interact much with the other kids.

Oops, I pissed all over myself and soiled my pants. I would have shit in them, too, if given half a chance.

What a joke! I know more than you. [This was the beginning of the interpretation of desire as knowledge-questing.]

The next several years were a complete waste, and ended up in frustration and anger. *What a cruel joke! I didn't want to be around the plotlines they had assigned me. What a pisser.*

Inebriating the white light until it was a piss-soaked, fuzzy yellow became my ratio decidendi for everything I did. Flash forward to a quanta of decades and I could barely remember anything except for the fuzzy-yellow. There was no ground, and even when I conned myself into a belief that there was, I sank in the quicksand of my assumptions. Unfortunately [and ironically], the better I got at understanding and manipulating the symbols of my culture, the more efficient the quicksand became.

We're just not sure what to do with him. His needs may be greater than we can provide, but we will try.

What a shame.

We're sorry to have to tell you.

Congratulations!

Excellent work—mostly—the rest is puzzling.

Goodbye, and good luck. Thanks for letting me know.

Enjoy your new life.

Please don't call.

Wow. What a move. That's amazing. Gutsy.

Hey, long time, no see.

I got to the edge of the desert and decided to fly back for the wedding. Everyone was there, which was both exciting and anxiety provoking. Everything was still uncertain, but we shook hands as men do, and the ice was broken. This is not to say that anything had been accomplished, but I did feel better.

Afterwards, he and I were able to share a few quiet moments, which gave us each the perception that our relation had survived the desert.

There was an opening that each of us seized, which allowed in the warmth of the sun and the reverberations of the refracting moon. Thus, there was at least the experience of a shared ontological wholeness while, even though fragmentary and ephemeral, left with it traces of good feelings.

After I left town, I took them with me, kept them, and therefore allowed myself to feel them whenever it felt like we were approaching again the desert.

In fact, after I woke up in back of the alley of the dive bar, my first thoughts were to call him, which I couldn't because he had long passed on to new dimensions and worlds. However, the imagination of Him brought me some comfort and a smile, even though I was full of pain. He would have said without saying something about being tough. I suspect this is partially why I had waited so long to get my diagnosis: I thought I could grit it out.

However, by the time I made it in to the doctor's—and at that point I no longer had health insurance, having retreated from the usual and customary bourgeois strategies—it was too late, and all they prescribe was kindness and palliatives.

That's how I ended up with her in an unexpected way at an unexpected time.

Between these two points, the desert of silence with Him and my later collapse that brought me to her, there was a cyclical pattern in which I grasped for an ontology that would bear my weight.

What I mean to say is that I wasn't a gambler or a boozer, or anything like that. I took my responsibilities seriously, and I just wanted something solid.

I wanted the solidity of a summer day—afternoon—warm sky—just enough clouds to count—dinner waiting and no rush to be there—the wind waiting and patient—the Indian Paintbrush standing guard, bearing witness to the stillness—the noise gone, my thoughts gone—everything motionless.

Thus, I tried everything I knew how for that solidity. Each

job. Each girlfriend. Each party. Each adventure.

Each breath I took was simply an attempt at that solidity.

My acceptances were rote, perfunctory, and alienated. My performances barely acceptable.

I danced to the logics and the words of each situation, my white light covered and protected, totally withdrawn from what was happening around me. At the time I believed that this strategy would ensure the continuity of that white light—and my authentic destiny.

I later learned that this strategy was responsible for keeping me in this interminable pattern. My regular visits home became less frequent, year after year, while my pattern was maturing.

Thus, the opening between him and me became narrow— perhaps more thin, as it were—and what little I knew of him eroded and dissipated until it became like the alienated experiences in the rest of my world.

Starting early, one of my favorite places to be in was the library. Any library, anywhere, as long as it had books, and the more books the better. I'd started going to them in grade school, and this pattern stuck throughout every revolution and evolution in my life, until I got sick and got nauseated by reading. I was always anxious about reading more.

Anyway, these patterns and nomenclatures and cycles continued past my twenties and thirties, and I grew older.

The seasons passed and I continued trying to find my position in all of it, my solidity.

Then, the pain started in my stomach.

would peek and poke their way into my path, without regard to the consequences—always seeking a way in and a way out.

Intriguing to me was my perception that the core of who I had become was separate and apart from the imaginings, thoughts, and behaviors I had routinized. I mean to say that I had a belief that I had an authentic core, a pure self that was a beacon even in dark nights and stormy skies.

I didn't feel responsible for what befell me on my path through life, and I came to realize that the beacon—the inner light—was an algorithm of my destiny. It never failed me even in times of immense stress or conflict.

Retrospectively, I was always able to look back and say *that was for the best*, even though the ride might have been rough. What I learned was that if I could stay detached from my persona—my personal identity—and meet the road with openness, mindfulness, and great awareness, all was a bounty of joy even through tears and hardship.

Like the sun just hanging its fingers over the clouds in the west at the end of the long day, the inner light always hung on safe and untainted.

There were those times that I tried to deconstruct it, make it less than it was; I even led myself to believe that it was illusion: a light of illusion! Yes, it persisted even in my darkest hour and even in the greatest confusion.

There it was, the light.

So I made my way as a young man and aged. How was I to navigate the uncertainties? My temporal nature? [the blasted problem of death and dying]; morality was a jungle, and we were all pushed from day one to accept the dialectic of the True and the Right.

I would only notice it right when I woke up and then later in the afternoon, and I tried all kinds of remedies and analgesics—teas, pills, capsules, diets—whatever sounded good; and I think that any relief I had was more about trying something new, pushing my system in different directions. Controlling the pain in a variety of ways and means created pathways in my sense of freedom, so I always appreciated finding new ways to push up against that solidity, to taste it even as it escaped me.

The jobs and the relationships changed towns and changed faces.

I became more aware of details, and more aware of myself, which I grew to accept. This made it easier to engage in these transformations even as my pain grew worse. New York, L.A., Atlanta, Chicago: they all hurt. The Midwest and the South bored me. The mountains froze me. I put a lot of miles on my cars, never stopping, always moving to my next.

And I'd always return from the desert of my existence.

How-r-ya doing, he'd ask, by phone.

Ok, I'd say.

Then we'd talk about the weather.

And every time I got off the phone I came up with a number of questions I'd wanted to ask him but didn't. Then these, too, would erode and dissipate until I forgot them from the first instance.

"Authenticity," "living the authentic life," and other informal aphorisms, I carried with me like candy and I'd pull them out as I needed. I didn't want to confront the fact that I'd all but given up on the hunt for these life ideals, preferring instead to live my cycle and my patterns.

It was a familiar life and brought me closer to that solidity that I craved.

So there it was, the oscillation between the translucence of the white light and the confusions of the symbolic; the struggle between the "transcendent" and the complicated structures of every day life. It was this struggle that provided fuel for my path, each offering relief to the other, neither a complete respite.

There was the trip across the country where we learned of each other's patience and tolerance.

There was his incredible ability to listen.

There was his agreeable attitude.

There was his wry and complicated sense of humor.

There were the short, punctilious questions.

There was his minding his own business. This was the flip side of the lack of knowledge problem: by avoiding the space that would inherently lead to sado-masochistic dynamics, he created both peace and a lack of intimacy. This was the price that we both paid, but it resulted in peace.

When he passed away, I felt a number of things, but what I focused on mostly was the nausea.

This was caused by the relaxing of the threads of dialectic in which I had been constructing meaning from my adolescence. He passed and I gained perspective.

It was a time of rain—the years that directly followed—being washed over clean.

This led to a new perspective about solidity and its real

possibilities. Unfortunately, this was tainted and distorted by the disease that had taken over my life. Releasing myself from the constraints we had woven in the symbolic had only led to a greater awareness of the fragility of my life—and the suffering. As my experience of solidity became fuller, in a corresponding way the acuity of my suffering became more pronounced.

I was dying.

I woke up one morning—at least two years after—one early spring day, to the rain pelting against the roof.

I got up and sat on the couch in the living room.

It was dark still, and everyone else was still asleep.

As the dawn advanced and the early rays of the sun penetrated through the curtains, I was struck with a déjà vu about my life—that not only had I been here before but that I had already, always been here. In one moment I was able to transcend past, present, and future, by both looking back from now, and by looking forward from then—all at the same time.

What are you doing with your life?

Your behavior reflects on me, you know.

Is this what you want on your permanent record?

I see things differently from you.

I have a different path.

This is important to me.

[Silence permeated the desert of our relation. Even after

we re-approached each other well into my adulthood, there was still a fulcrum of it, thick and heavy, from which we would engage each other. Even after he was gone, it was here, especially in the room with me now. His admonitions and reprisals still hung in the air forcing me into a resistant dialectic, defending, tensing, remembering.]

There's nothing there.

What about the future? Don't you think things can change?

[The stony silence crept in and he didn't answer. This was his way.]

Fortunately, as he grew older he replaced the silence with positive commentary; this is not to say that he became engaging, but he did offer his perspective, which gradually overtook the thick and heavy.

Now that he was gone, that silence had re-emerged into all things in the symbolic, all matters at home, and in the lion's share of my thoughts.

He was present even in death and quite ironically had only begun his retreat as my disease took hold and the pain dominated all of my experience.

Do you have any advice for me? [I fought harder to stay in the dialectic.]

What's important? What have you discovered? What do you know?

Not a thing. [This was unbelievable to me. "Nothing?"]

[It pissed me off, in fact, his seeming unwillingness to share his insights about life with me, but there was nothing I could do.]

At one point I had started deconstructing my quest for wisdom, for the answers he seemed unwilling to provide.

I searched for others that I could fashion myself after, to no avail—it was my desire for his knowledge and his wisdom that I wanted, no one else's.

As I aged, I was able to separate my feelings for him from whom I thought he was. Now, one might object that this mental maneuver would be impossible—I would have argued the point—until I experienced it.

I watched others who spoke with him; listened attentively; imagined I was not his issue; and through these exercises came not only to see him in a new light but to actually appreciate the artistic, unique iteration that he was. In exchange, I was able to relax my vise grip on the reactive mode I was living in relative to Him.

The cascade effect of this relaxation emerged from my confrontation with the asymptotic decrease in sedimentation: I was able to approach the pure ontological field of possibility, which brought both exhilaration and anxiety, intertwined with my disease, in a mobius strip of complexity. This caused me to reach back for him but it was futile; the tie had been cut.

There were tears in my eyes when it happened—when he left.

That was until he gave me that look in the cemetery.

He gave me that look from across the lawn as we lowered his body into the earth. He looked into my eyes and smiled; he did this as he walked away, deliberately, gently, on his own return. It was then that my pain took on new depth and intensity.

They took me to the hospital later that day.

Part

Three

There was the darkness.

There was a familiarity in the darkness though I strained to make out who it was.

It was quiet—like being home in the middle of the day, sounds outside, muffled, but none that quite penetrated. Except for the dripping water.

Ting—-. Ting—-. Ting. Then it stopped, and I heard footsteps.

It was all darkness in here, along with that muffled silence, until she shuffled in. It had been a while, a very long time, but I could tell who it was from the way she stepped down the hall. Gentle and deliberate, she approached while I lay there unmoving.

~~~

It was difficult to make out what was happening.

There was an enclosure, and enclosures within that one. It was all so dark, and I could hear a great deal of scuttling about. Of course, I had no idea what this was all about, except that I was at the center of attention—everything focused.

They were preparing me for entry and, as such, had to provide me with the covering and the appearance that I would assume for the duration.

It was hard to see, and I didn't understand much except for the most concentrated aspects of what was happening in my immediate space.

Curiously, I realized years later—when the light came into my mind—that I hadn't chosen any of it; my sole job was to deal with it.

This is a curious sort of experience, in which you have a modicum of awareness, usually incomplete, and you are forced along a certain path in a certain way. Here, the degree to which you comply is often viewed as a sign of your native intelligence. Total non-compliance is seen as evil or lacking in "smarts."

Anyway, there was all this preparation: pushing, advising, introducing—scuttling about to get ready. Then the day came and I arrived, my soul old and experienced in these matters, my body nascent, young, new.

It was still unclear what my mission was this time around, something that would only be clear through time; this was part of it, learning about the aim and focus of this phase of the journey.

What was more intriguing and challenging was that, according to the logic of the system, my awareness of what had been before—any wisdoms that I might have accumulated—would gradually dissipate until I remembered nothing. And so it was, this problem of human beings constantly and perennially forgetting everything they had ever learned.

The darkness. The quiet.

The solidity of their entangling became the foundation for my "safe zone." This was the place of utter repose—from still to still, dark to dark, and a life plan of which I was unaware.

Unfortunately, after my stay in the unknown dark sea— which I later learned was a womb—I came face to face with the stark, stank brightness of the sun. Along with the requirement that I had to fit in to this complicated morass of anxiety, noise, confusion, I had few resources with which to organize my experience.

There were fragments of noise and slivers of light; there were non-understandable exchanges between her and me.

On occasion, He would hold me, but there was no rhyme or reason to any of his or her behaviors and, as such, it was unpredictable.

To allow myself attachment this messy conundrum was terrifying. To avoid attachment was horrific, and equally terrifying. Thus, I was in a position of precarious ambiguity, with no core. I wasn't even an "I."

Years later I could recall the yellow paint, the evening arguments—which at that time emerged as cacophony, the stillness in the air but unfortunately *this stillness had nothing to look forward to, and it was not comforting in any way. It was a deathlike closure, waiting to explode the walls of the prison-like container at the beginning. I remembered this all too well years later, in my early 60s when they brought me to her in my transition process.*

Look how cute he is.

What a beautiful baby.

Such a beautiful boy; don't you think he has his grandfather's eyes?

[They were in part looking for my reaction and in part, not. I was not yet cognizant enough to care, but there was a lot of fuss—constantly. As I grew in awareness I did learn that they were imploring my reaction, out of need for power, driven by their own ontological "issues." For me, it FELT forced, that I was obligated to respond. To the extent I did not, I was met with disapproval. To the extent I gave them the face they wanted, I earned credits.]

[This was much like the paradoxical trauma I would later face as I lay dying, in which I would trade off solidity for painful freedom. This feeling, though, of being forced, created in me an aggressive animus that both helped and hindered me throughout the rest of my life, perhaps in equal proportion, but I couldn't know it then/now, since I was only an infant. The main thing was that to gain my-Self, my identity, I had to pay the price of "being" forced. This, then, became a pillar of my own ontological structure; being forced.]

[Thus, my freedom of movement, its very ratio, was in part reactive and un-free. To remain distant from my own self, then, was both free and un-free; it was free in the sense that I refused being pinned by their gazes, un-free in the sense that I was split off, anchored in the deep, dark cosmos of my own alienation—my ontological closet.]

How! How beautiful!

My only respite became the dark bedroom between the graying evening and the yellowing morning, and the occasional "nap" in between. But the respite was good enough to motivate me toward its sweet relief, over and again.

Bright spears coming through the window.

He had left a little while ago so it was quiet now.

One might consider this a time of peace—comfort from the silence, full belly, mama in the room, but it was more of a black hole pulling everything into it without permission. He was only gone because he had to work; she was only here because it was her job. The black and white television on the kitchen counter competed with the old AM radio, but this wouldn't happen until lunchtime, which was supposed to be some sort of exciting thing.

Meanwhile, *I was impressed over and over by the imperative to "learn the ropes," never quite "getting it," palpably noticing the split between what was expected of me and who I was in actuality. It was a constant interplay between the vacuousness of my infancy and the implicit demands of the situation into which I had been delivered. This is not the deliverance of salvation; rather, it was the stress and tension of deliverance to a facticity that I had not chosen, nor would I have ever.*

Someone in the family died when I was very young—I don't remember who it was.

This was just a taste, and as I grew older I could see with more perspicacity the great numbers of those "passing away." It always reminded me of blades of just cut grass being thrown over the sharp steel shank that propelled all life forward. Bourgeois life that is.

Then it happened again when I was a bit older and I still didn't understand. Totally perplexed I asked all the usual questions, but mostly I considered the possibility of my non-being, which was beyond me because there was nothing that I could predicate. It was a possibility that was beyond my comprehension.

I kept a notebook in my head, recording my memory—the folks I knew who died.

In the early years, it was my older relatives, and an occasional accident. In the middle years, there were more accidents and some suicides, along with the aging passing away.

When I was young—just coming into consciousness—the whole matter greatly perplexed me. I thought that they must have gone somewhere, and simply would not accept the possibility of permanent termination. This belief coincided with my experience of pets dying and friends moving away: they simply went somewhere else; and even though this created sadness, I could live with it, wrap my head around it. However, as time passed, I was struck with the quickness of the turnover.

I would visit cemeteries, take pictures, drink beer, smoke cigarettes, sit on the grass. I'd lie back in the afternoon and stare at the sky while allowing the blades of grass in the necropolis to comfort me like a down pillow and a feather bed.

I knew it wouldn't be long.

The point was that, back in the early days when I was navigating the gaze of the other, trying to make my way in a world that I had no part in fashioning, I had a real problem with the fact that it was all over sooner than one could plan for. This made me believe that the joke was on those who pretended that what was, was all. I played it differently and, as such, had a difficult time fitting in to the "program."

Everything was relative and relational: the draw of a certain family in a certain time in a certain place would determine my outer fate. Nevertheless, because I was able to hold back and keep protected that eternal part of me that had always been, I knew I became more of an observer; a participant-observer who knew better.

The yellow of the kitchen was so easy to remember perhaps because this is where we spent most of the time.

It took me years to recall the color of the bedroom—it was a sort of light, swarmy green, not a light green, not forest, but the sort of green you might find on the walls of a one-star European hotel. Paint that had been there forever, absorbing smoke, fire, passion, death, and broken dreams.

This is where I slept, and I will always remember the funky little lamp she'd put in the room; it illuminated a rounded little patch on the wall where I could see anomalies of paint chipped and cracked over the years. It was a rental and we were just tenants passing through, another round of the blades of grass that were sliced and laid to rest before the rakes collected them into the garbage, later fertilizing another living space for others.

Thus, there was a concatenation of fragmented images, sounds, smells, feels, and tastes—the rules unclear and shifting.

Another child came along, and then another, thus the "high-chair" got passed down, as did the "wisdom" from the older ones to the younger.

My basic orientation was ambivalence, as I explained, between my still core [my masochism] and the "liberating" movements of my forays into the symbolic [my sadism], as it came to me.

I didn't want to give myself away to their bad faith, nor their own ontological disasters, but the stillness of my own isolated, "inner" core would have driven me insane had this been my only position-without dialectic.

People argued about this, I later discovered, whether there was such a "core." Maybe this was a protective illusion that allowed us to cope with being forced into a facticity that we never chose and could never take back. Maybe this is what made people selfish later, when they had an irrefutable instinct to take, to covet, and to hoard.

Inevitably this resulted in a gloating sort of intentionality in which competition for scarce resources was the norm. In my own family, for instance, this manifested in gamesmanship for perceived love. I later learned that the ironic shadow of receiving it only resulted in an ongoing enslavement in order to maintain it.

The dusty dirt road at the beginning.

The railroad trestles at the bottom of the rise.

The station wagon that we used for family trips.

The yellow and the green. Cheap carpet and throwaway furniture.

Occasionally, outsiders who invaded the quietude of the morning or family friends who invaded it in the afternoon.

Sunlight lighting my way, as I became aware of the Big Circumstance at play. Again, in retrospect, I wondered even then, as I became aware, that there was an antagonistic pull against the teleology into the future: I'd come from somewhere that continued to seem preferable to the cliff from which I was falling.

Obligations and demands, more cacophony, the two of them hashing it out as I was shuffled back and forth from the shadowy green into the sun-lit yellow, and occasionally let out into the yard and onto the hill, sometimes going for rides in the station wagon.

YES and NO became the double instruments of oppression

and development, infusing everyone around me with unique combinations of sadistic and masochistic energy.

Bath time was relief, especially when the warmth of the bubbles overcame the pressures of the day; for just those few moments I gained respite—but not for long because I felt the pull from the other direction backwards from wherever I had come.

Mostly it was the confinement that defined the situation—and each of us. It was gothic in the sense that we had our encapsulated reality away from all other realities.

Smells were the usual: the shit of the day. Just washed and dried clothes from the used washer we'd gotten by charity. Coffee. "Mush," which was a cheap version of oatmeal. Cheese. "Goolash." "Casserole."

Soup.

~~~

Cacophony.

Feeling forced into a theatre with logics and rules that someone else chose. The whole matter was such pressure, and I felt like I was dying every time I assented to their admonitions and encouragements.

Here, like this. Do it like this!

You mustn't.

Good boys always do such and such and so forth. You want to be a good boy, don't you?

The pressure and demand was so overwhelming I had no words for it, just a concatenation of disorganized raw emotion.

[Standing on a white sandy beach one day, years later, feeling a light breeze flow right through me, I was able to recall the pressure that I had felt. The solidity of that time period suffocated me, pushed up against me hard until I had nowhere to turn.

I was being molded, in part intentionally and in part unconsciously. Nonetheless, I was being shaped in ways that I tried to understand for the rest of my short life, even as I lay dying decades later.]

"Even as I lay dying." *The words I ran through my mind at the end, and yet I would also say them in retrospect when I thought about the early years. During that early period, of course, I didn't have the words to think of anything, and even as my awareness grew into language, I continued to form and refine the concept: As I lay dying perfectly described my experience of my entry into culture and family.*

They tried their best to kill me off. I suppose why I became a nay-sayer, a Contrarian, and a freedom fighter. I resisted all of it, which many tried to explain in terms of the Good and the Right, or the True and the False—as time passed.

I wanted to go back inside myself and back to wherever I had come from but I had no idea how to do this and no idea how to think about it. This caused me the greatest of distress, which no one understood. As such, I was viewed as recalcitrant and intractable, and they were all concerned for me.

I experienced greater and great levels of their desire to suck me into their way, their culture, their customs, and their ontological satisfactions. At the time, my only recourse was retreat into a conscious hibernation as a method to survive their ministrations.

The yellow and the green made me sick.

The railroad inveigled me, almost to the point of my being run down by a locomotive.

The yellow light rays never made it very far into the house, dissipating once they reached the edge of the kitchen. This left the rest of the place shadowy and gray, and a little split off from the rest of the world.

The smells were of small children—poop, pee, vomit. Cheap kid food. Coffee.

Cigarette smoke that had furtively entered through the front door from when she'd go out to "hang the clothes."

When He'd come home, there would be the sound of his car keys hitting the counter. Excitement in the air. A bit of chaos. The smell of dinner. A bit of rough housing. But it was all over so quickly: the tempo came in these quick bursts, so we rarely got our fill and were always left wanting.

Then the dinner, usually some level of cacophony. Then he'd go out, to smoke, I think. Then we'd go into the gray dark of the green-colored room.

Weekends changed that tempo. He'd wake late and we'd have been fed. Then we'd go somewhere. I remember the car moving and all. Sundays were with church and grandparents.

Before all this initial theatre there was just the yellow and the green and the shadowy, smokiness. Alternating with the feeling of being forced was the nesting—being placed in various ways in accordance with some plan that I struggled to learn.

The solidity was stifling. Moving was free, but wasn't much

allowed. Its appearance was illusory, and I wanted so much to return from wherever I had come. It was torment. Sad and full of tears. Being forced into it all, without my assent.

The railroad tracks were deliverance, a symbol of ontological space where possibility always ruled over what was actual.

~~~

It was typical for there to be a familiarity in the darkness though I would strain to make out who it was.

Usually it was quiet—being home in the middle of the day, sounds outside, muffled, but none that quite penetrated. Except for the dripping water.

Ting—-. Ting—-. Ting. Then it would stop, and I would hear footsteps.

It was all darkness in here, along with that muffled silence, until she would shuffle in. It always seemed like it had been a while, a very long time, and I could tell who it was from the way she stepped down the hall. Gentle and deliberate, she approached while I lay there unmoving.

The water came on full into a pan or a bowl. Something clicked on and a sliver of yellow light forced its way into the muffled dark. It was just enough to startle me but not enough to irritate my tired, sore eyes.

The right I kept closed, the left open just enough to en-frame the darkness, the narrow slit of yellow and, in conjunction with my ears, the running water.

Then the water trickled out and ended.

I would normally have expected to hear a voice coming from

the movement just on the other side of the door and the yellow pencil of light, pointing its way through the entrance. But sometimes she didn't say anything and continued with the running water, padding toward me carefully carrying a bowl, until she creaked the door open.

First the hardwood floor creaked then the door. It was torment and grace simultaneously.

He was gone.

And I thought I could hear a humming sound coming from somewhere else.

Post

Script

I felt the life slip out of me as I became more aware, growing in consciousness, having these realizations.

~~~

My body was now deeply sunken into the ground—dead— but I had been able to reach out my hand forward, open and grasping in unison with his eyes trained carefully on me as I drew into the future.

With unknown strength and love I stretched out my hand, my arm drawn its full length, my eyes open pools of gratitude. It was the hand of love that I had opened that caused such joy. I had given absolutely everything to get him here to this point. I had given everything.

Even in the dry burning heat, the sticky tears dripped down from my eyes. I continued looking beyond my open hand and saw him raising his own. As I raised my hand, looking, holding my arm and my hand outstretched, joining, across that nothingness, his eyes—my eyes—started to close.

And my hand fell to the ground.

As my hand fell to the ground, my eyes closed from the heat and the dizziness and the gratitude.

Then I heard another voice calling from an unknown place in the dark, across the yellow of the sun—

Look for the follow-up story...

The
Return

Kevin Boileau

Heart-of-Fire

Heart-of-Fire is an imprint of EPIS Press dedicated solely to fiction, poetry, and other literary production that is related to psychoanalysis, phenomenology, and Critical Theory/ deconstruction.

EPIS Press
31 Fort Missoula Road
Suite 4
Missoula, MT 59804
epispublishing1@gmail.com
www.episworldwide.com

www.ingramcontent.com/pod-product-compliance
Lightning Source LLC
Chambersburg PA
CDIIW070605100626
46817CB00005B/2010